Literature Circle Guide:
Julie of the Wolves

by Perdita Finn

S C H O L A S T I C
PROFESSIONAL **B**OOKS

New York • **Toronto** • **London** • **Auckland** • **Sydney**
• **Mexico City** • **New Delhi** • **Hong Kong**

Guide written by Perdita Finn
Edited by Sarah Glasscock
Cover design by Niloufar Safavieh
Interior design by Grafica, Inc.
Interior illustrations by Mona Mark
Copyright © 2001 by Scholastic Professional Books. All rights reserved.

ISBN 0-439-16359-5

Printed in the U.S.A.

Contents

To the Teacher

As a teacher, you naturally want to instill in your students the habits of confident, critical, independent, and lifelong readers. You hope that even when students are not in school they will seek out books on their own, think about and question what they are reading, and share those ideas with friends. An excellent way to further this goal is by using literature circles in your classroom.

In a literature circle, students select a book to read as a group. They think and write about it on their own in a literature response journal and then discuss it together. Both journals and discussions enable students to respond to a book and develop their insights into it. They also learn to identify themes and issues, analyze vocabulary, recognize writing techniques, and share ideas with each other—all of which are necessary to meet state and national standards.

This guide provides the support materials for using literature circles with *Julie of the Wolves* by Jean Craighead George. The reading strategies, discussion questions, projects, and enrichment readings will also support a whole class reading of this text or can be given to enhance the experience of an individual student reading the book as part of a reading workshop.

Literature Circles

A literature circle consists of several students (usually three to five) who agree to read a book together and share their observations, questions, and interpretations. Groups may be organized by reading level or choice of book. Often these groups read more than one book together since, as students become more comfortable talking with one another, their observations and insights deepen.

When planning to use literature circles in your classroom, it can be helpful to do the following:

✳ Recommend four or five books from which students can choose. These books might be grouped by theme, genre, or author.

✳ Allow three or four weeks for students to read each book. Each of Scholastic's *Literature Circle Guides* has nine sections as well as enrichment activities and final projects. Even if students are reading different books in the Literature Circle Guide series, they can be scheduled to finish at the same time.

✳ Create a daily routine so students can focus on journal writing and discussions.

✳ Decide whether students will be reading books in class or for homework. If students do all their reading for homework, then allot class time for sharing journals and discussions. You can also alternate silent reading and writing days in the classroom with discussion groups.

Read More About Literature Circles

Getting the Most from Literature Groups by Penny Strube (Scholastic Professional Books, 1996)

Literature Circles by Harvey Daniels (Stenhouse Publishers, 1994)

Using the *Literature Circle Guides* in Your Classroom

Each guide contains the following sections:

✱ background information about the author and book

✱ enrichment readings relevant to the book

✱ Literature Response Journal reproducibles

✱ Group Discussion reproducibles

✱ Individual and group projects

✱ Literature Discussion Evaluation Sheet

Background Information and Enrichment Readings

The background information about the author and the book and the enrichment readings are designed to offer information that will enhance students' understanding of the book. You may choose to assign and discuss these sections before, during, or after the reading of the book. Because each enrichment concludes with questions that invite students to connect it to the book, you can use this section to inspire students to think and record their thoughts in the literature response journal.

Literature Response Journal Reproducibles

Although these reproducibles are designed for individual students, they should also be used to stimulate and support discussions in literature circles. Each page begins with a reading strategy and follows with several journal topics. At the bottom of the page, students select a type of response (question, prediction, observation, or connection) for free-choice writing in their response journals.

◆ Reading Strategies

Since the goal of the literature circle is to empower lifelong readers, a different reading strategy is introduced in each section. Not only does the reading strategy allow students to understand this particular book better, but it also instills a habit of mind that will continue to be useful when they read other books. Questions from the Literature Response Journal and the Group Discussion pages are always tied to the reading strategies.

If everyone in class is reading the same book, you may present the reading strategy as a mini-lesson to the entire class. For literature circles, however, the group of students can read over and discuss the strategy together at the start of class and then experiment with the strategy as they read silently for the rest of the period. You may want to allow time at the end of class so the group can talk about what they noticed as they read. As an alternative, the literature circle can review the reading strategy for the next section after they have completed their discussion. That night, students can try out the reading strategy as they read on their own so they will be ready for the next day's literature circle discussion.

◆ Literature Response Journal Topics

A literature response journal allows a reader to "converse" with a book. Students write questions, point out things they notice about the story, recall personal experiences, and make connections to other texts in their journals. In other words, they are using writing to explore what they think about the book. See page 7 for tips on how to help students set up their literature response journals.

1. The questions for the literature response journals have no right or wrong answers but are designed to help students look beneath the surface of the plot and develop a richer connection to the story and its characters.

2. Students can write in their literature response journals as soon as they have finished a reading assignment. Again, you may choose to have students do this for homework or make time during class.

3. The literature response journals are an excellent tool for students to use in their literature circles. They can highlight ideas and thoughts in their journals that they want to share with the group.

4. When you evaluate students' journals, consider whether they have completed all the assignments and have responded in depth and thoughtfully. You may want to check each day to make sure students are keeping up with the assignments. You can read and respond to the journals at a halfway point (after five entries) and again at the end. Some teachers suggest that students pick out their five best entries for a grade.

Group Discussion Reproducibles

These reproducibles are designed for use in literature circles. Each page begins with a series of discussion questions for the group to consider. A mini-lesson on an aspect of the writer's craft follows the discussion questions. See page 8 for tips on how to model good discussions for students.

◆ **Literature Discussion Questions:** In a literature discussion, students experience a book from different points of view. Each reader brings her or his own unique observations, questions, and associations to the text. When students share their different reading experiences, they often come to a wider and deeper understanding than they would have reached on their own.

The discussion is not an exercise in finding the right answers nor is it a debate. Its goal is to explore the many possible meanings of a book. Be sure to allow enough time for these conversations to move beyond easy answers—try to schedule 25–35 minutes for each one. In addition, there are important guidelines to ensure that everyone's voice is heard.

1. Let students know that participation in the literature discussion is an important part of their grade. You may choose to watch one discussion and grade it. (You can use the Literature Discussion Evaluation Sheet on page 33.)

2. Encourage students to evaluate their own performance in discussions using the Literature Discussion Evaluation Sheet. They can assess not only their own level of involvement but also how the group itself has functioned.

3. Help students learn how to talk to one another effectively. After a discussion, help them process what worked and what didn't. Videotape discussions, if possible, and then evaluate them together. Let one literature circle watch another and provide feedback to it.

4. It can be helpful to have a facilitator for each discussion. The facilitator can keep students from interrupting each other, help the conversation get back on track when it digresses, and encourage shyer members to contribute. At the end of each discussion, the facilitator can summarize everyone's contributions and suggest areas for improvement.

5. Designate other roles for group members. For instance, a recorder can take notes and/or list questions for further discussion. A summarizer can open each literature circle meeting by summarizing the chapter(s) the group has just read. Encourage students to rotate these roles, as well as that of the facilitator.

◆ **Writer's Craft:** This section encourages students to look at the writer's most important tool—words. It points out new vocabulary, writing techniques, and uses of language. One or two questions invite students to think more deeply about the book and writing in general. These questions can either become part of the literature circle discussion or be written about in students' journals.

Literature Discussion Evaluation Sheet

Both you and your students will benefit from completing these evaluation sheets. You can use them to assess students' performance, and as mentioned above, students can evaluate their own individual performances, as well as their group's performance. The Literature Discussion Evaluation Sheet appears on page 33.

Setting Up Literature Response Journals

Although some students may already keep literature response journals, others may not be sure just what to write about in these journals. To discourage students from simply writing elaborate plot summaries and to encourage them to use their literature response journals in a meaningful way, help them focus their responses around the following elements: predictions, observations, questions, and connections.

Have students take time after each assigned section to think about and record their responses in their journals. Sample responses appear below.

◆ **Predictions:** Before students read the book, have them study the cover and the jacket copy. Ask if anyone has read any other books by Jean Craighead George. To begin their literature response journals, tell students to jot down their impressions about the book. As they read, students will continue to make predictions about what a character might do or how the plot might turn. After finishing the book, students can re-assess their initial predictions. Good readers understand that they must constantly activate prior knowledge before, during, and after they read. They adjust their expectations and predictions; a book that is completely predictable is not likely to capture anyone's interest. A student about to read *Julie of the Wolves* for the first time might predict the following:

I think that Miyax/Julie is a very strong girl. The book jacket says she runs away, she gets lost, and she makes friends with wolves. Looking at the illustrations in the book gave me a real feel about how hard it would be to survive in the Arctic. It must have taken a lot of patience and trust for her and the wolves to get close.

◆ **Observations:** This activity takes place immediately after reading begins. In a literature response journal, the reader recalls fresh impressions about the characters, setting, and events. Most readers mention details that stand out for them even if they are not sure what their importance is. For example, a reader might list phrases that describe how a character looks or the feeling a setting evokes. Many readers note certain words, phrases, or passages in a book. Others note the style of an author's writing or the voice in which the story is told. A student just starting to read *Julie of the Wolves* might write the following:

I notice she's only thirteen years old, and she's married! I wonder if that's why she runs away. I notice that the wolves seem very friendly and like a big family. Miyax is all by herself. She talks about her father, but she doesn't seem to mention her mom.

◆ **Questions:** Point out that good readers don't necessarily understand everything they read. To clarify their uncertainty, they ask questions. Encourage students to identify passages that confuse or trouble them, and emphasize that they shouldn't take anything for granted. Share the following student example:

How did Miyax end up in the tundra all by herself? How did she survive this long? Isn't she scared being all by herself? Will she find food to eat? I wonder if the wolves will take her in to live with them.

◆ **Connections:** Remind students that one story often leads to another. When one friend tells a story, another friend is often inspired to tell one, too. The same thing often happens when someone reads a book. A character reminds the reader of a relative, or a situation is similar to something that happened to him or her. Sometimes a book makes a reader recall other books or movies. These connections can be helpful in revealing some of the deeper meanings or patterns of a book. The following is an example of a student connection:

I keep thinking about The Jungle Book *and how Mowgli was raised by wolves. It almost feels like this wolf family is going to adopt Miyax.*

The Good Discussion

In a good literature discussion, students are always learning from one another. They listen to one another and respond to what their peers have to say. They share their ideas, questions, and observations. Everyone feels comfortable about talking, and no one interrupts or puts down what anyone else says. Students leave a good literature discussion with a new understanding of the book—and sometimes with new questions about it. They almost always feel more engaged by what they have read.

◆ **Modeling a Good Discussion:** In this era of combative and confessional TV talk shows, students often don't have any idea of what it means to talk productively and creatively together. You can help them have a better idea of what a good literature discussion is if you let them experience one. Select a thought-provoking short story or poem for students to read, and then choose a small group to model a discussion of the work for the class.

Explain to participating students that the objective of the discussion is to explore the text thoroughly and learn from each other. Explain to the whole class that it takes time to learn how to have a good discussion, and that the first discussion may not achieve everything they hope it will. Duplicate a copy of the Literature Discussion Evaluation Sheet for each student. Go over the helpful and unhelpful contributions shown on the Literature Discussion Evaluation Sheet. Tell students to fill out the sheets as they watch the model discussion. Then have the group of students hold its discussion while the rest of the class observes. Try not to interrupt or control the discussion, and remind the student audience not to participate. It's okay if the discussion falters, as this is a learning experience

Allow 15–20 minutes for the discussion. When it is finished, ask each student in the group to reflect out loud about what worked and what didn't. Then have the students who observed share their impressions. What kinds of comments were helpful? How could the group have talked to each other more productively? You may want to let another group experiment with a discussion so students can try out what they learned from the first one.

◆ **Assessing Discussions:** The following tips will help students monitor how well their group is functioning:

1. One person should keep track of all behaviors by each group member, both helpful and unhelpful, during the discussion.

2. At the end of the discussion, each individual should think about how he or she did. How many helpful checks did he or she receive? How many unhelpful checks did he or she receive?

3. The group should look at the Literature Discussion Evaluation Sheet and assess their performance as a whole. Were most of the behaviors helpful? Were any behaviors unhelpful? How could the group improve?

In good discussions, you will often hear students say the following:

"I was wondering if anyone knew . . ."

"I see what you are saying. That reminds me of something that happened earlier in the book."

"What do you think?"

"Did anyone notice on page 57 that . . ."

"I disagree with you because . . ."

"I agree with you because . . ."

"This reminds me so much of when . . ."

"Do you think this could mean . . ."

"I'm not sure I understand what you're saying. Could you explain it a little more to me?"

"That reminds me of what you were saying yesterday about . . ."

"I just don't understand this."

"I love the part that says . . ."

"Here, let me read this paragraph. It's an example of what I'm talking about."

About *Julie of the Wolves*

Survival stories have always captured the imaginations of readers—whether it's a thrilling account of scaling Mount Everest, an epic journey across the frozen South Pole, or *Julie of the Wolves*. In this captivating story, a young girl is lost in the vast Arctic tundra with the endless darkness of winter approaching and only wolves to rescue her. Whether you enjoy learning about animals or discovering a completely different way of life—or you just love adventure—this is a book that offers a remarkable glimpse of another world.

About the Author: Jean Craighead George

An often-repeated rule of writing is "to write what you know." What's amazing about Jean Craighead George is that she's actually experienced many of the same things as the characters in her books! She's spent time in a seal camp in Alaska, eaten blubber and caribou, and dressed like an Eskimo to keep warm in Arctic temperatures; she's spent time with the wolves, getting to know them and "talking" with them in their own language.

Jean Craighead George's parents were naturalists, and they would take her and her brothers into the wilderness along the Potomac River near their home in Washington, D.C. Their father taught them about the animals, where to find edible plants, and how to make shelters to sleep in and fish hooks from twigs. The children even learned how to train falcons, and her brothers became the first falconers in the United States. Jean's first pet wasn't a cat or a dog, but a turkey vulture. She writes about her childhood:

I learned much, and had come to feel close to the natural world. I still thrill to the memories of shooting the murky rapids of the Potomac on a big sycamore log, and jumping from boulder to boulder along the gorge. And there were the quiet, intimate hours spent on the forest floor looking at insects, a garden of moss, or a bird.

By the age of six, Jean knew she wanted to be a writer, and after majoring in English at Penn State College, she became a reporter for the *Washington Post* and a member of the White House Press Corps. Meanwhile, she was bringing home animals like owls, robins, minks, sea gulls, and tarantulas to her three children. George estimates that she's had over 173 pets (*not* including cats and dogs!). Many of these pets have become characters in her books.

One summer Jean went to Barrow, Alaska, to write a magazine article on wolves. As she and her son Luke flew into the Barrow airport, they happened to see a young Eskimo girl out on the tundra. Luke remarked that she "looked awfully little to be out there all alone."

At the Arctic Research Lab in Alaska, Jean learned how friendly wolves actually were, and she met scientists who were beginning to break the animals' communication code. Jean herself was soon able to talk with a beautiful female wolf. She realized that she wanted to write about these wonderful, misunderstood creatures and, remembering the girl she had seen, began imagining the story of a lone young girl who is saved by the wolves.

Since writing *Julie of the Wolves*, Jean has had many more opportunities to spend time with wolves. Recently, she went to Utah, where wolf pups were being raised to star in the movie version of *Julie of the Wolves*. She fed Silver beef soup, gave Amaroq a bottle, and held Nails in her arms while he slept. She's also been back to Alaska, where her son Craig now studies whales. Her experiences with the native peoples there inspired George to write *Julie*, a sequel to her award-winning book.

When Jean Craighead George writes, she always thinks about how much children love nature. More than anything, she hopes that her books will make them "want to protect all the beautiful creatures and places" of the world.

Enrichment: The Yupik of Alaska

Alaska became a state in 1959, but other than a blurred vision of seals, igloos, and Eskimos, many Americans know little of the native people who have lived there for thousands of years.

The word *Eskimo* was once used for all the groups of people living in the Arctic. Each of these groups was very much defined by the available natural resources. Native Alaskans fall into two groups, the Inupiat in the north and northwest and the Yupik in the southwest and on St. Lawrence Island.

The Yupik people made their homes along the southwest coast with its abundant resources, including sea and land animals, waterfowl, and fish. Since there were few trees in the harsh environment, the Yupik traditionally built their houses, or *qasgiqs*, half underground. They would find a dry area, dig down, build a wooden structure that projected from the ground, and then cover it with earth and sod. In the same manner, they would build a tunnel to the doorway of their dwellings, which helped to keep in precious warmth.

The Yupik believed that sea mammals, such as walruses, seals, and whales lived in huge underwater *qasgiqs* where they arranged themselves around a fire pit in order of importance. From their homes, the mammals watched the world of people and decided whether or not to give themselves to human hunters.

Like many Native American peoples, the Yupik both hunted and honored the animals around them. For the Yupik, all living beings had spirits and were equally sacred. Animals were important for sustaining their life—for providing meat for food, fur for clothes, bones for tools—and the Yupik believed the animals might disappear if they weren't treated with respect.

The Yupiks wore masks, or *agayu*, and performed dances as a way of praying to the animals so they would come when they were hunted. The Yupik would wear walrus masks and mimic the sounds walrus make, as if they were actually becoming that animal. They felt that the spirit of the animal was entering them when they danced. Many *shamans*, or spiritual leaders, had special wolf masks that were representative of their helping spirits. They would call on the wolf when they needed special help curing someone in the community. The Yupik thought the wolf was particularly powerful because it is bold and can capture whatever it pursues. One Yupik elder has said that the wolf only comes to those it knows are clean and pure. She suggests that people ask what would be improved in the community if they could call on the power of the wolf.

Since oil was discovered in Alaska, the Yupiks' way of life has changed. Less than a quarter of the population of Alaska today is native inhabitants, and the traditional Yupik way of life has been radically transformed. Many now live in modern villages. They work for schools, stores, commercial fishing operations, and the government. Still, there are Yupik people today who live as their ancestors did; they hunt, fish, and gather berries and eggs. They speak their own language and dance together and hold elaborate community gift-giving ceremonies (*potlatches*).

Contemporary Yupik authors are publishing books about their traditional way of life, and Yupik artisans continue to create the traditional crafts for which they are famous. What else would you like to find out about the Yupik? What have you found out about them from reading *Julie of the Wolves*?

Enrichment: Wolves

The wolf lies in wait for Little Red Riding Hood. He blows down the three little pigs' houses. A werewolf howls at the moon. From earliest childhood, we are taught to fear this animal above all others. Its fangs are huge, its claws are sharp, and it will devour anything in its path—or will it?

In the 1940's, a young scientist named Farley Mowat was sent to the Canadian Arctic by the Canadian Wildlife Service to gather evidence that wolves were destroying the caribou population. Hunters had been complaining about decreased herds and wanted to carry out a massive extermination of wolves. What Mowat discovered, however (and wrote about in his wonderful and funny book called *Never Cry Wolf*), was that the wolves mostly ate mice and an occasional sick or old caribou. In fact, wolves helped keep the caribou herds strong and healthy. The only real danger to the caribou (and the wolves), it turned out, were people who hunted them and built settlements in what had been the animals' vast feeding grounds. Mowat fell in love with the wolves, with their skill as protectors and providers for their families.

Most wolves in America have been hunted to extinction, although the gray wolf and the Mexican wolf have begun to make an appearance in the lower states again. The Arctic wolf is the purest breed of wolf and has probably survived because it lives in the isolated area around the Arctic Circle.

Wolves are not nearly as big as people imagine, but are about the size of a German shepherd. They do not fight unnecessarily and will often go out of their way to avoid conflict. Wolves are social animals, and every wolf in a pack knows its position. There is an alpha, or dominant, male and an alpha female, and they usually mate for life. All members of the pack show great care and affection towards the pups. Some wolves even serve as baby-sitters! Wolf packs are typically extended families of five to eight wolves but can have as many as 20 members.

Wolves are meat-eaters, and they can hunt game with keen efficiency, relying on their remarkable senses of smell and hearing. They eat five to ten pounds of meat a day and wash it down with water and grass. They'll eat moose, deer, rabbits, ducks, and even fish and insects—almost any animal that presents itself at a disadvantage—although there still remain many questions about exactly which animals wolves will eat and why.

Being hunters themselves, the Yupik people had great respect for the wolf and its abilities. They honored the wolf and hoped that it would share its secrets with them. For most Europeans, who were farmers and herders (and from whom our fairy tales come), the wolf merely represented a threat to their livestock. Many of the settlers who came to America wanted to tame the wilderness rather than let it exist or flourish.

If you begin to study any animal, you will discover that its behavior, relationships, and place in the ecosystem are much more complicated and subtle than you might have thought. What have you learned about wolves by reading *Julie of the Wolves*? What else would you like to find out?

Enrichment: Shamans

Traditionally among Native American people is the belief that everything—every animal, plant, rock, and mountain—has a spirit within it that must be honored. In order to understand those spirits and communicate with them, Native Americans usually designate one person in the community as a *shaman*. Part priest, part doctor, and part scientist, the shaman (which literally means "he who knows") takes care of the whole community by assuring that the animals hunted are paid due respect and will therefore continue to offer themselves to killed, healing sickness using herbs and animal lore, and passing along the many stories that define the traditional beliefs and customs of their people.

For the Yupik, the shaman is someone who knows the paths of the fish and the caribou, their patterns, and when to perform certain rituals to encourage the animals' arrival. In fact, because they are so observant of the world around them and have inherited much traditional wisdom, some modern biologists have sought out shamans for their insights into the natural world.

The shaman is someone who can move between two different worlds—the physical, day-to-day world of hunting and cooking and living, and the unseen spirit world. Birds (which also move between heaven and earth) are often associated with shamans. Pre-scientific people believed that everything was caused by the spirits—illness, the availability of animals to hunt, the weather, people's relationships—and thus the shaman's ability to speak and intervene with that spirit world was very important.

Some shamans are born into their roles, but in most groups, certain people are recognized in childhood or adolescence as having special powers of awareness. Usually, when the future shaman is a teenager (and among the Yupik it might be a boy or a girl), he or she feels a special calling and may be sent alone into the wilderness on a vision quest or journey of self-discovery. During the vision quest, the teenager experiences hardships and may come close to dying, but may acquire an animal guardian (or totem) who will give him or her power. Sometimes the guardian even leaves an amulet—some kind of picture of itself that can be used for protection. Eventually the shaman must return from the vision quest and the world of spirits to the ordinary world in order to serve.

The deep respect that shamans have for the natural world has inspired many modern environmentalists interested in protecting endangered plants and animals. Is there anything about the shaman's way of looking at the world that you find particularly interesting? How does Miyax in *Julie of the Wolves* come to understand the shaman's role in her community?

Name _____ **Date** _____

Julie of the Wolves
Before Reading the Book

Reading Strategy: Background Knowledge

Julie of the Wolves takes place in the frozen tundra of Alaska, a setting few readers are likely to have visited. The author describes the place with much detail, but before you begin to read, it can be helpful to look at some pictures that will help you develop an image in your mind. Check out a book on Alaska from the library, consult an encyclopedia in the library or on the Internet, or visit a Web site. Look at the vast tundra at the Arctic Circle. Can you imagine being by yourself there? How do you think you would feel?

Writing in Your Literature Response Journal

A. **Write about one of these topics in your journal. Circle the topic you chose.**

1. Carefully describe an experience you have had in nature. Perhaps you were camping or just out for a walk or a hike. What kinds of plants and animals did you see? What was the weather like? Explain what your experience was like.

2. What is the longest time you have ever spent alone? Where were you, and what did you do? How did it feel to be alone? Did you feel lonely? If so, what kinds of things did you do to make yourself feel better?

3. Write about an animal you know well—perhaps a pet or a creature in the wild you have observed. How does this animal "talk" to you? How do you know when it's hungry, when it wants to go outside, when it's angry or happy? How does it behave around other animals? What have you learned about this animal from watching it?

B. **What were your predictions, questions, observations, and connections about the book? Write about one of them in your journal. Check the response you chose.**

❏ Prediction   ❏ Question   ❏ Observation   ❏ Connection

Literature Circle Guide for *Julie of the Wolves* • Scholastic Professional Books

Name _____ **Date** _____

Julie of the Wolves
Before Reading the Book

For Your Discussion Group

When we begin reading a new book, we bring our prior knowledge and experiences to it. Sometimes this helps us imagine what we are about to read, but sometimes it can keep us from being open to new ideas or fresh perspectives. Before we read, it can be helpful to think about what we know about certain subjects. In this way, we can open our minds, or even change them.

❋ Working individually, make a list of what you know about wolves. What are the first things that come into your mind when you think of these animals? What stories do you associate with them? What have you heard about their behavior? What would you do if a wolf were in your back yard?

❋ Next have everyone share his or her thoughts. You may want a group member to record your collective ideas. Have you expressed the same kinds of things as other members of your circle, or do people have different attitudes about wolves? Discuss the similarities and differences in your attitudes.

❋ Read the first paragraph from *Julie of the Wolves*. What is the first thing you notice about these wolves? Does it correspond to what you thought about wolves or does it surprise you in some way? Explain your reaction.

❋ Share with your circle what you know about the native peoples of Alaska and how they live. Record your ideas. Some of what you know will be inaccurate, and some will prove to be true. As you read the book together, return to your list and note which things prove to be false and which prove to be true.

Literature Circle Guide for *Julie of the Wolves* • Scholastic Professional Books

Name _____ **Date** _____

Julie of the Wolves
Part I: Pages 5–23

Reading Strategy: *In Medias Res*

Most fairy tales usually begin with the words "Once upon a time," and start at the very beginning of the story. Some stories start in the middle of things, or *in medias res.* Some movies open this way as well: the hero is running away, but we don't know who is chasing him or her, or why, until later in the story. Many traditional epics begin this way, for instance, with an enormous war already underway. Storytellers do this because *in medias res* gets the reader instantly involved in the story.

When you read a story that begins *in medias res,* it is important to remember that there may be things you do not know. That's okay. Your questions will eventually be answered.

Writing in Your Literature Response Journal

A. Write about one of these topics in your journal. Circle the topic you chose.

1. Think about other books or stories you have read or movies or television shows that begin *in media res.* Choose one, and compare its beginning to the beginning of *Julie of the Wolves.*

2. Miyax is lost on the tundra. How does she behave? What do you notice about her? What would you do in that situation? Have you ever been in a life-threatening situation? What did you do? Compare yourself to Miyak. How are you like or different from her?

3. Write down some sentences from the book that really gave you a picture of where Miyax is and how it feels to be there. Now go outside and describe your surroundings. Notice colors, textures, any animals, the sky, and all the sights, sounds, and smells around you.

B. What were your predictions, questions, observations, and connections about the book? Write about one of them in your journal. Check the response you chose.

❏ Prediction   ❏ Question   ❏ Observation   ❏ Connection

Literature Circle Guide for *Julie of the Wolves* • Scholastic Professional Books

Name _____ Date _____

Julie of the Wolves
Part I: Pages 5–23

For Your Discussion Group

✻ Most of the characters in this book are animals. This can be difficult for a reader to get used to. As a group, make a list of all the different wolves in the pack and discuss what each one is like. Just as Miyax imagines that one is like her father and another is like her stepmother, imagine the wolves are like your family and friends. Who does Silver remind you of? Who do Jello and Kapu bring to mind?

✻ In the midst of this account of Julie's first encounter with the wolves are some clues about why she is on the tundra and what her life was like before. Individually, list what you noticed about Julie's prior life. Then have everyone in the group share his or her list and pool your knowledge.

Writer's Craft: Appositives

When a writer introduces an unfamiliar name or idea, she or he will often immediately define or describe it further. That definition or description is often set off by commas and is called an **appositive**. In writing about an unfamiliar place and way of life, Jean Craighead George uses a lot of appositives.

She spoke half in Eskimo and half in English, as if the instincts of her father and the science of the gussaks, the white-faced, might evoke some magical combination that would help her get her message through to the wolf.

As you read, notice the appositives. Try using some appositives in your own writing to make your thoughts clearer and more specific!

Name _____   Date _____

Julie of the Wolves
Part I: Pages 23–49

Reading Strategy: Conflict

Jean Craighead George says that when she is writing
a story she first thinks of a main character and then
thinks of a problem she wants that character to solve. In fact, most stories are about
problems or conflicts and how the characters resolve them. As you read, notice what
some of Miyax's conflicts are. Some, you will notice, are resolved during the course of
the story, while others will not be resolved until the story's conclusion.

Writing in Your Literature Response Journal

A. Write about one of these topics in your journal. Circle the topic you chose.

1. Record the conflicts and problems that Miyax experiences in this section of the
book. How might she resolve these conflicts and problems? As you read, compare
your solutions to Miyax's solutions.

2. Kapugen gives the following advice to Miyax:

*"Change your ways when fear seizes," he had said, "for it usually means you
are doing something wrong."*

What do you think of this advice? Does it work for Miyax? Would it work for
you? Write about a time when you were afraid and tell how you could have
"changed your ways."

3. Miyax treats the wolves as her family, but in doing so, she must eat other animals,
including the baby owls that she finds. What does Miyax think about eating animals?
How does she treat the animals she eats? What would you do if you were in her position?

**B. What were your predictions, questions, observations, and connections about the
book? Write about one of them in your journal. Check the response you chose.**

❑ Prediction   ❑ Question   ❑ Observation   ❑ Connection

Literature Circle Guide for *Julie of the Wolves* • Scholastic Professional Books

Name _____ **Date** _____

Julie of the Wolves
Part I: Pages 23–49

For Your Discussion Group

✻ In order to survive, Miyax relies on the traditional Eskimo lore she learned from her father. She also finds herself beginning to honor some of the old traditions, such as the song of the Bird Feast. Talk about where your families originally came from and what traditions you know about. What are some of the traditions centered on food, growing up, or the seasons? Like Miyax, which ones are you uncomfortable with? Which ones do you like to celebrate? Which ones would you like to know more about?

✻ Remember how important it is to honor and respect differences among each other in your group. Make sure that all the members of your group feel comfortable sharing their thoughts and ideas.

Writer's Craft: Words in Context

It is not always necessary to stop reading to look up unfamiliar words in the dictionary. We can figure out the meanings of new words from how they are being used. If we understand the rest of the sentence (or paragraph), then often we can use that information, or the **context**, to make sense of the unfamiliar word. For instance, the author describes how Miyax performs the following task:

> *[She] plucked the birds, laid them on the ground, and skillfully cut them open with her ulu. Lifting out the warm viscera, she tipped back her head and popped them into her mouth. They were delicious—the nuts and candy of the Arctic.*

Viscera may be a new word for you, but you were probably able to tell it means the organs of the body from context clues. Study the following words in context to determine their meanings: *regurgitated* (page 32), *deference* (page 33), and *apogee* (page 49).

Literature Circle Guide 101: Julie of the Wolves Scholastic Professional Books

Name _____ Date _____

Julie of the Wolves
Part I: Pages 49–70

Reading Strategy: Making Comparisons

If you place two apples next to each other, you will find that you suddenly notice more about each apple. You'll notice which one is bigger, harder, redder, and which one has a longer stem. Making comparisons is an important way of observing. When you read, you may want to compare two characters. Think about how they are the same and how they are different.

Writing in Your Literature Response Journal

A. Write about one of these topics in your journal. Circle the topic you chose.

1. What do you discover when you compare Miyax and the wolves? What surprises you most about the similarities and the differences you find?

2. Miyax is learning a tremendous amount from the wolves. Write down some of the things she has learned. In what way does Miyak's personality allow her to learn so much? Has there ever been a time when you learned from some person, animal, or situation? What did you learn?

3. Miyax is an excellent observer of the animals around her. Like an expert naturalist, she knows how to wait and be patient. Pick an animal to watch, such as a pet, insect, bird, or wild animal. Take time to really watch it. Be as still as possible as you observe. Then record your observations.

B. What were your predictions, questions, observations, and connections about the book? Write about one of them in your journal. Check the response you chose.

❏ Prediction   ❏ Question   ❏ Observation   ❏ Connection

Literature Circle Guide for *Julie of the Wolves* • Scholastic Professional Books

Name _____ Date _____

Julie of the Wolves
Chapter I: Pages 49–70

For Your Discussion Group

✳ *Julie of the Wolves* is a book filled with the rhythms of nature and all the varieties of emotion that Miyax experiences. If you were a musical composer, how would you express the different feelings and moods within the first part of this book?

✳ Pick a passage in the book that you love, and find a piece of music that expresses the emotion of the words.

✳ Share your passage and music with the rest of your group. Explain why you chose the music and what you discovered about the words in the passage when you set them to music. (You may want to talk with your teacher about providing a cassette or CD player.)

✳ As different group members share their passages and music, how do you respond to their choices? What do you learn about the book from listening to the different kinds of music your group chose?

Writer's Craft: Verbs

Verbs are the action words in sentences. They give writing energy and specificity. For instance, Jean Craighead George writes, "The sky vaulted above her," instead of "The sky above her was like a vault." The first sentence is tighter and much more powerful because of the verb she uses. As you read, notice the verbs that George uses, such as *splotched, inched, stifled,* and *blotted.* Which verbs stand out for you?

Name _____ **Date** _____

Julie of the Wolves
Part II: Pages 75–88

Reading Strategy:
Adjusting Your Reading Speed

A lot of readers worry about how slowly they read. While it is important to read quickly enough to get the full meaning of what you are reading, it is also valuable to slow down and linger over the words. Poetry is always better read slowly. Say the words aloud, taste them. Writing that has the flavor of poetry is also worth savoring. Read some of the descriptive passages in this section slowly out loud to yourself, and listen to how they sound. Do you hear the music of the sentences?

Writing in Your Literature Response Journal

A. **Write about one of these topics in your journal. Circle the topic you chose.**

1. Which passage or passages did you choose to read slowly and savor? How did it affect your understanding of the story? How did your appreciation of the author deepen or change?

2. Miyax remembers scenes from her life in the seal camp as "beautiful color spots." Imagine scenes from a specific time in your life as color spots, too. What are your gold memories? Which memories are blue or green? Write about at least five different color spots from your life.

3. What if you were Julie's new pen pal? What would you write to her about your life? What would you want to ask her about her life? Now write a letter to Julie.

B. **What were your predictions, questions, observations, and connections about the book? Write about one of them in your journal. Check the response you chose.**

❏ Prediction   ❏ Question   ❏ Observation   ❏ Connection

Literature Circle Guide for *Julie of the Wolves* • Scholastic Professional Books

Name _____ **Date** _____

Julie of the Wolves
Part II: Pages 75–88

For Your Discussion Group

✳ Begin your discussion today by having everyone in the group pick one sentence that he or she loves. Then have each person share that sentence, without explaining why he or she chose it and without any commentary from the group.

✳ As you listen to the sentences, what do you notice? Have some people picked the same sentence? (They may, since certain sentences will be particularly powerful.) Or has everyone selected a different sentence?

✳ After you have shared your sentences, discuss them. What kinds of feelings is the story bringing up for you at this point? What are you thinking about as you read? What questions are you asking?

Writer's Craft: Names

As the passage below shows, Jean Craighead George understands how powerful names are.

With that Miyax became Julie.

When we change our names—because of marriage, a new religious affiliation, or for personal reasons—it usually means that we are changing who we are in some sense. When a little boy announces he no longer wants to be "Tommy" but "Tom," he is telling everyone he wants to be treated less like a child. How many different names do you have? Do your parents and friends have nicknames for you? What's in a name? What does it tell about you? Is there a name you wish you had?

Name _____   Date _____

Julie of the Wolves
Part II: Pages 88–104

Reading Strategy: Visualizing

At one point, Julie shuts her eyes and imagines
the world of San Francisco that Amy has
described for her. As a reader, she is making a
conscious effort to visualize the words from the
letters. Good readers often visualize while they read. They create pictures in their minds.
Take a moment in the midst of your reading and pay attention to what you are imagining.

Writing in Your Literature Response Journal

A. Write about one of these topics in your journal. Circle the topic you chose.

1. Visualize the main character and the setting of the story. What does Julie look
like? What does the house she lives in look like? Describe the environment in
which she lives.

2. Each section of this book is about a journey that Miyax, or Julie, takes. Where
does she begin in Part I, and where is she at the end? Where does she come from
in the second part, and where is she going? As you describe Julie's journeys, draw
a timeline to show how she travels and changes.

3. Write about one of your own journeys, either an important trip you took, or a
time when you moved or were experiencing a lot of changes. What happened to
you during that time? What did you learn about yourself and other people?

**B. What were your predictions, questions, observations, and connections about the
book? Write about one of them in your journal. Check the response you chose.**

❏ Prediction   ❏ Question   ❏ Observation   ❏ Connection

Literature Circle Guide for *Julie of the Wolves* • Scholastic Professional Books

Name _____ **Date** _____

Julie of the Wolves
Part II: Pages 88–104

For Your Discussion Group

❋ Writers are always making choices about which details to include in their work and which to leave out. Discuss with your group why Jean Craighead George might have chosen to include the detail below in her description of Julie's escape from Barrow.

No one was on the street but a single tourist who was photographing the sun in the sky.

❋ In order to help you think about this, you will need to look at what else George says earlier in the book about Barrow, the Eskimos there, and the sun. You will also need to think about what Julie is running away from and what that could have to do with this seemingly insignificant detail.

❋ Remember that different members will have different opinions and ideas about the significance of this passage. There is no single right answer to such a question.

Writer's Craft: Similes and Metaphors

Jean Craighead George describes the houses in Barrow as being "like a cluster of lonely birds" and Julie as an "eagle seeking out new pinnacles." In order to help readers visualize what they are describing, writers use comparisons to help create a clearer picture. **Similes** are comparisons, such as the description of Barrow above, that use the words *like* or *as*. **Metaphors** are comparisons, such as the description of Julie above, that describe something as if it were actually something else. One thing you will notice about Jean Craighead George's similes and metaphors in *Julie of the Wolves* is that she only uses things for comparison that you would find in Alaska, such as lonely birds and eagles. What other comparisons do you find as you read?

Name _____ **Date** _____

Julie of the Wolves
Part III: Pages 109–129

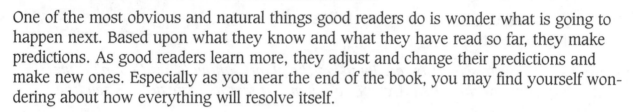

Reading Strategies: Making Predictions

One of the most obvious and natural things good readers do is wonder what is going to happen next. Based upon what they know and what they have read so far, they make predictions. As good readers learn more, they adjust and change their predictions and make new ones. Especially as you near the end of the book, you may find yourself wondering about how everything will resolve itself.

Writing in Your Literature Response Journal

A. **Write about one of these topics in your journal. Circle the topic you chose.**

1. What do you think is going to happen to Julie? What will happen to the wolves? What other things are you wondering about? Record your predictions.

2. To occupy her while she works, Miyax sings songs of praise about her wolves. They are simple yet powerful. Read the song on page 116 a few times. Then write your own song about something you love. Like Miyax, you may want to sing it as you make it up!

3. Make a list of all the factual information you know about Jello. After you look over your list, think about why he is troubling Miyax. What do you think he has against her? Was there any other way Miyax could have dealt with Jello? Explain your reasoning.

B. **What were your predictions, questions, observations, and connections about the book? Write about one of them in your journal. Check the response you chose.**

❏ Prediction ❏ Question ❏ Observation ❏ Connection

Literature Circle Guide for *Julie of the Wolves* • Scholastic Professional Books

Name _____   **Date** _____

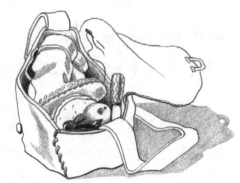

Julie of the Wolves
Part III: Pages 109–129

For Your Discussion Group

✻ Divide your group into two teams and debate the following quote:

The Eskimos were scientists too. By using the plants, animals, and temperature, they had changed the harsh Arctic into a home, a feat as incredible as sending rockets to the moon.

✻ One team should argue in favor of the quote; the other should argue against it. (It doesn't matter if you *actually* agree or not. The purpose for each team is to explore one side of the issue.) Each team should find support for its point of view from the book itself. Search for quotes and make note of specific scenes.

✻ When all of you have collected your supporting information, each team takes turns presenting evidence. Select one person to record the evidence.

✻ Then, as a group again, talk about the quote. What is your personal opinion of the quote? Do you agree or disagree with it? Has your view shifted since the debate? If it has, explain how and why. Remember—you can change your mind; it shows that you're thinking.

Writer's Craft: Sentence Variety

The season had been brief; the flash of bird wings, the thunder of migrating herds. That was all. Now it was winter, and the top of the soil was solid. No blue sea would be lapping the shores of Barrow; instead the Arctic Ocean would be a roaring white cauldron forming icebergs that would join the land with the polar cap.

A simple rule of writing is to vary the length of the sentences you write. If all the sentences are the same length, it can become monotonous; if some are short and others long, the words have more rhythm. In fact, you can even think of punctuation like musical notation; for example, a period is a full stop, while a comma or a semicolon is a short pause. Read the above passage, and notice the variety in the sentences.

Name _____ **Date** _____

Julie of the Wolves
Part III: Pages 129–151

Reading Strategy: Asking Questions

You don't have to understand everything you
read. In fact, good readers ask questions and pay
attention when they are confused or troubled by something that happens in a story.
While you read, write down questions about the things you don't understand. Record the
questions in your journal or bring them to your group discussion. Remember—the more
questions you ask, the more deeply you will begin to read.

Writing in Your Literature Response Journal

A. **Write about one of these topics in your journal. Circle the topic you chose.**

1. How did you feel about what happened to Amaroq? Did it surprise you? Explain
   your response. Do you think you would have felt the same way at the beginning
   of the book? How have your feelings about wolves changed since then?

2. On page 134, Kapugen describes the "interconnectedness" of the different Arctic
   animals, or what biologists call "the web of life." Draw a picture of what he
   explains so you can visualize it more clearly. Then think about the plants and
   animals in your own environment. How do they depend on each other? Write
   about what you have noticed.

B. **What were your predictions, questions, observations, and connections about the
book? Write about one of them in your journal. Check the response you chose.**

❏ Prediction ❏ Question ❏ Observation ❏ Connection

Literature Circle Guide for *Julie of the Wolves* • Scholastic Professional Books

Name _____ **Date** _____

Julie of the Wolves
Part III: Pages 129–151

For Your Discussion Group

✸ Where do you think Miyax should go next? Tell why. What do you think she will do? If you could advise Miyax right now, what would your group want to say to her?

✸ In her grief, Miyax asks the spirit of Amaroq to enter the carving she has made of him. In this way, she feels he is still with her. What kinds of things do you do when you are sad or missing someone? How is it the same as what Miyax does? How is it different?

Writer's Craft: Word Derivations

As people have migrated around the world, they have brought their languages with them. Many English words actually come from, or are **derivations** from, other languages. From the English colonization of India, we get such words as *bungalow*, *jungle*, and *curry*. German immigrants gave us *kindergarten*, *ecology*, and *phooey*. From the Yupik people of Alaska come such words as *igloo*, *parka*, and *ulu*. Look up a familiar word in the dictionary and find out from which language it originally comes. What other words in *Julie of the Wolves* do you think are originally from Yupik?

Name _____ **Date** _____

Julie of the Wolves
Part III: Pages 151–170

Reading Strategy: Making Inferences

What happens at the end of *Julie of the Wolves*?
There will be some specific events you will be able to
point to—she sings a song, she heads back to Kapugen—but in order to figure out what
these events *mean*, you will have to do some thinking. Jean Craighead George, like
many good writers, doesn't explain everything for her readers. She says one or two simple things, and allows her readers to fill in the rest of the story, to make inferences about
the bigger picture.

Writing in Your Literature Response Journal

A. Write about one of these topics in your journal. Circle the topic you chose.

1. What really happens at the end of this story? What does it mean when Tornait
dies? Why does Miyax head back to her father? Is the ending happy or sad?
Record your inferences. Explain how you made the inferences, and include evidence from the story.

2. Read the following passage from the story:

*There the old Eskimo hunters she had known in her childhood thought the riches
of life were intelligence, fearlessness, and love. A man with these gifts was rich
and was a great spirit who was admired in the same way that the gussaks
admired a man with money and goods.*

When is Miyax the richest? According to Eskimo wisdom, when is her father the
richest? What do you think of this definition of wealth? Do you feel wealthy or
poor? Explain your reasoning. Would Miyax think you were rich?

**B. What were your predictions, questions, observations, and connections about the
book? Write about one of them in your journal. Check the response you chose.**

❑ Prediction   ❑ Question   ❑ Observation   ❑ Connection

Literature Circle Guide for *Julie of the Wolves* • Scholastic Professional Books

Name _____ **Date** _____

Julie of the Wolves
Part III: Pages 151–170

For Your Discussion Group

✴ The ending of this story is ambiguous: nothing is spelled out for you, and you are left to figure out for yourself what it means. Nevertheless, there are certain events in the story that indicate how Jean Craighead George wants the reader to feel about Miyax and her future. Discuss the ending of the story: is it happy or sad? Justify your reasoning.

✴ As you read, think about the significance of the death of Miyax's bird, her father, of the song she sings at the end, and also of the title of the book itself. Why is it called *Julie of the Wolves* and not *Miyax of the Wolves*?

✴ The conclusion to this story is very open. What does your circle imagine happens next? Write the next two or three pages of the story. If you want to really challenge yourself, try and make it sound like Jean Craighead George's writing!

Writer's Craft: Specialized Vocabulary

Whenever you read about a new topic, you are sure to learn new words because every subject has its own **specialized vocabulary**. What new words have you learned while reading *Julie of the Wolves*? Think of words that describe the environment, such as *tundra* and *lichen*; words that describe animal behavior, such as *dominant* and *deference*; and words about the Alaskan people, such as *totem* and *parka*. Many of these words will be so familiar to you by the end of the book that you may not even realize they have become part of your vocabulary. Take a minute and think about all the new words you have acquired through reading this story.

Julie of the Wolves
After Reading

Jean Craighead George saw a young girl wandering on the tundra near Barrow, Alaska, and began to imagine her story. Like all writers, she infused her story with what she cared about most—animals, the environment, and the conditions of native peoples. On the one hand, George is spinning a story to entertain her readers; on the other, she is offering an education on issues important to her. What did you learn when you read this book? Did it change your mind about anything?

✳ Brainstorm in your journal using the following starter:

Before I read this book, I thought _____.

Now I think _____.

✳ Try to complete at least ten pairs of these sentences. Then put a star next to the one you feel is the most important to you.

✳ Divide a large sheet of unlined paper into three parts. In the first part, show what you used to think. In the third part, show what you now believe. You may use text, draw pictures, create collages, or do some combination. Be as creative as you want.

✳ Finally, in the second part, write about what it was in *Julie of the Wolves* that changed or opened your mind. It might be a scene from the book or a quote or some dialogue, or it might be a combination. Record all of them.

✳ What if you think you didn't learn anything from the book? First, ask yourself if that's really true. Isn't there a new thought about yourself and your life, about Miyax and her situation, that you'd never had before? Maybe you learned about a new kind of animal or a new kind of food to eat. Even when we don't realize it, we are learning things at every moment.

✳ Share your responses with your literature circle.

Literature Circle Guide for *Julie of the Wolves* • Scholastic Professional Books

Individual Projects

1. Learn more about wolves. Make a list of questions you still have about them, and begin reading and researching. *Of Wolves and Men* by Barry Lopez and *Never Cry Wolf* by Farley Mowat are two books you might enjoy. The Internet also has many interesting sites on wolves. Once you've found the answers to some of your questions, you may want to present them in a report or, like Jean Craighead George, use your new knowledge in a story.

2. As Jean Craighead George knows, the best way to learn about animals is to spend time with them. Many areas now have wildlife rehabilitators who heal and return hurt animals of all kinds back to their natural habitats. (Even New York City has falcon rehabilitators because of its enormous peregrine population, so don't assume there aren't any in your area if you live in a city.) Often you can contact the rehabilitators through a local animal welfare group, veterinarian, or the local police. What can you find out about the wild animals in your environment?

3. Classrooms all over the world are looking for pen pals! At Epals [http://epals.com], you can write kids from Native Alaskan schools.

- -

Group Projects

1. Contact the local chapter of the Sierra Club, the Audubon Society, Greenpeace, or other environmental groups in your area to find out about some of the environmental issues where you live. You may want to do some research on the Internet and in the newspapers to broaden your understanding of what's happening. Each member of your group might contact or research a different environmental organization and then report back to the group. Together you might then decide on how to get involved in helping your local environment.

2. Research the traditional ways of the Yupik people. Some group members may want to research hunting, others may study family life, and some may have an interest in arts and crafts or storytelling. Everyone can produce an object from her or his research—a copy of a traditional mask, a tool the Yupik used at one time, a diorama of a village, and so on. Include a description of the object's purpose.

Literature Circle Guide for *Julie of the Wolves* • Scholastic Professional Books